WALAHADLI

PARISH TWO

PARISH ONE

Opal Island

DUSABE

Isaiah Dusabe — Georgina Westiwa

Joanna Suvan — Edmond Dusabe

Seven Dusabe

Contessa Dusabe

OPA

KWADIO

Thomas Kwadio —— Tabitha Kwadio

Rene Kwadio

Isola Kwadio

ISLAND

Published by Bee Infinite Publishing
Los Angeles, CA

ISBN 978-1-7360038-6-2
www.beeinfinite.org

Printed in the United States of America
First Printing, 2023

Opal Island

Opal Island

by Amina Lovell

infinite publishing
LOS ANGELES

Book One

~ 1 ~

RENE

Thomas shuffles through some documents on his desk when Rene storms into his office. "You still haven't signed the papers. Why not?" She folds her arms roughly and narrows her eyes. Thomas casually gets up from his oakwood desk and looks out of the window directly behind him. "While I appreciate your ambition, Rene, we can't breach the barrier. It is forbidden."

Rene scoffs loudly. "Are you still talking about the fairy-tale creatures, grandfather? Because I'm bored of this conversation already." She takes a few more steps into the room, her face set in a contemptuous snarl. "Sign them, it's what's best for the Parish."

"Who do you think built that barrier?" Thomas challenges. "We don't know what else they have created, or how dangerous they have become," he sits back in his chair. "I will not sign them; you have no idea what you're doing."

Rene grins widely. "I know more than you and the board of directors. Twenty old men, paranoid about fiction from the past. We finally have the technology to tear it down, and it's time to face whatever is on the other side. We can beat them, whatever they are."

"That technology came from the barrier, and we still don't fully understand it," Thomas says, annoyed. "We have no business using it for our own gain."

"I have made contact with Nessus," Rene says casually, ignoring Thomas's frustration. "They want to see it, and see how we've developed it. Once we tear down the barrier we will have the entire island and unlimited trade value with Walahadli."

Thomas shakes his head firmly. "I see you've been scheming...again," he huffs loudly, looking at Rene with disappointment. "I will not sign this, we have no reason to go back there, no reason to engage with them ever again. The answer is no, Rene."

"It's no longer a request," Rene spits back, maneuvering slowly to his bookshelf as she gazes cruelly towards her grandfather. "I'm done asking for your permission," she pulls a diamond-shaped humanitarian award from the top shelf, gripping it in her hands tightly.

"You're not going to stop me," she says.

Thomas quickly opens his top desk drawer. Pulling out a gun, he aims it at her chest. "I don't want to kill you, but I must protect the Parish. Your parents, the Divine rest their souls, entrusted me to look after you. Don't make me do this."

"I'd really be scared if that gun had bullets in it," Rene says, sauntering slowly towards his desk. She turns the award around in her hands over and over, feigning playfulness. Thomas points the gun at her chest and pulls the trigger a few times. It makes a loud clicking sound. He throws the gun back into the drawer, frantically rummaging for something else.

"If you're looking for your letter opener, that's gone too," Rene circles around the desk, holding the award firmly in her hands, she points the end at her grandfather, making her intentions clear. Thomas jumps up from his chair, reaching for a pen on his desk. Rene smacks it away, trapping him up against the wall. "You brought this on yourself." Before Thomas can say anything else, Rene violently shoves the award into his chest. He stumbles to the side, reaching for and missing his desk. He falls on his back, Rene pulls the award from his chest and mounts his bleeding body. She drives the edge of the award into his chest, again and again, soaking her clothes in warm blood. Thomas tries to speak but only spits up blood, groaning in pain. Rene pushes the sharp glass into his chest one more time, splattering more blood all over the wall and the desk.

She stands up and throws the award on the floor, taking a deep breath as she smiles at the dead body lying before her.

"Old, simple, superstitious. The Parish is better off without you."

Rene calls her head security officer into the room. "Jonathan, clean this up," she commands. "Make it look like a violent break-in, then schedule an emergency board meeting tomorrow with all twenty members. We're moving ahead."

CONTESSA

"Do you want to talk about it?" Chelsea asks in a concerned tone over the phone. "I know you said it isn't a big deal, but your birthday is *always* a big deal."

Tessa cradles her cell phone between her ear and shoulder, putting the final touches of nail polish on her toenails. "I honestly don't know if talking about it will help, Chels. I know it's going to be extra weird this year because of the induction ceremony. I'm positive they forgot all about it."

"Don't say that, you don't know what they have planned, maybe they'll make a toast or something?" Chelsea says hopefully.

Tessa scoffs loudly. "Yeah, a toast to the disappointment and "freak of nature" they call a daughter."

"Well, technically, you aren't a freak of nature and that's the problem, right?" Chelsea laughs.

Tessa can't help but smirk. "True, maybe they'll finally tell me I'm adopted so we can just stop this charade."

Chelsea lets out a hearty chuckle. "So, *dramatic.* You look exactly like your parents, so I doubt it."

Shoot. I shouldn't have said that. Tessa thinks to herself. "Chels, you know I didn't mean it like th-" she tries to backtrack.

"It's fine, I know," Chelsea says quickly. "Now that we've graduated, we should start an anti-freak-of-nature-club, and form a whole new pack."

"I like it!" Tessa wiggles her toes, admiring her handiwork. "Better yet, let's start a band!"

"You read my mind," Chelsea squeals. "You know I'm getting really good at the iktala, I learned two new songs yesterday."

"Better than working in the marketplace," Tessa says. "We should move to the mainland after the summer. What's keeping us on Opal Island now?"

"What do you mean?" Chelsea asks.

"After graduation, everyone just picks up odd jobs or works for the council. But since we're not shapeshifters, maybe we should just...leave."

"Tessa," a soft voice comes through her door suddenly, "are you coming down to eat?"

"Chels, let me call you right back," Tessa ends her call, jumps off her bed, and opens her door. "Yes, I will eat up here Ms. Pryce. Can you bring it up to me?"

"Why don't you come downstairs and chat with me?" Ms. Pryce says persuasively. "I haven't seen you all day."

Tessa smiles. "I'm ok just getting ready for the big weekend ahead, I know there's a lot to be done."

"Yes, there is," Ms. Pryce says slyly. "You still haven't told me what kind of cake you would like me to make for you."

"Don't worry about the cake," Tessa says quietly. "We won't be making a big deal this year, I'm sure."

"Nonsense," Ms. Pryce says sternly. "It's not every day a young lady turns sixteen, we have to celebrate."

"We'll see," Tessa says, "I will take dinner in my room though. Let's talk tomorrow, okay?" Before Ms. Pryce can protest any further, Tessa slowly closes her door. A few moments later Ms. Pryce is back with a tray of food and cutlery.

"You can't hide in here all week, Contessa," Mrs. Pryce places the tray on her bedside table, setting out the cutlery neatly. "I know your birthday is a little touchy but you still have to celebrate it."

"The only people who get *touchy* about it are my parents," Tessa snips. "The great reminder that I'm not what they want me to be."

"Tessa, your parents love you, please come down and let's have a talk," Mrs. Pryce frowns at her. "You used to tell me everything, remember?"

"I do remember," Tessa says fondly. "You have cooked me every meal, read me stories before I went to bed, even came to my netball games. But you don't have to do that anymore, Ms. Pryce. I will be going to trade school soon. Before you know it, I'll be working. After all, it's time to grow up."

Ms. Pryce starts to say something but decides against it. "I understand. If you ever need anything, I'm always here." She walks out of the bedroom, closing the door behind her quietly.

Tessa turns towards her floor-to-ceiling window, taking in the night view of Parish One. *You were there because they couldn't be. They never could be.* She shakes her head, refusing to think about her past. Picking up her fork she digs into her dinner while calling Chelsea back. "Hey, sorry about that, I had to get dinner. So about this band, we'll need a lead vocalist."

JOANNA

The throbbing in her feet distracts Joanna from Edmond's question. She takes her time as she slips off her four-inch heels, massaging her ankles and feet after her Women's Empowerment Group meeting.

"Did you hear what I said?" Edmond asks from the balcony. "You have to come with me to find him, I don't remember anything of the ancient language."

"Yes, I heard you," Joanna says irritably. "I don't know why we have to adhere to this tradition anyway, it's not like he still converses with us."

Edmond walks into the bedroom, taking the last swig of his drink. "It took me too long to get to this point, to finally be the leader of the Parish. If I skip this, the council will have another reason to object to my induction." He sits next to her, rubbing her back slowly. Joanna leans into his massage, grunting her approval. "It will be quick."

"You know that's a lie," she says laughing. "He hates to be found and he's difficult to reason with."

Edmond stops rubbing her shoulders, he cups her face with his large hands. "Please," he asks meekly. "I can't do this without you."

No, you can't, I wish you would admit that more often. Joanna thinks to herself. "Ok fine," she finally says. "Let me put some comfortable shoes on."

A few moments later they walk downstairs into the kitchen. Ms. Pryce is putting on her sweater. "Going out?" she asks them curiously.

"Just for a few minutes," Edmond says smoothly. "We have a late meeting."

She nods knowingly. "Of course, it is almost time, you must meet him."

"Maria, has Tessa eaten? I haven't seen her all day." Joanna asks.

"She has," Maria says. "I think she's on the phone right now, very excited about her big day."

"You mean the ceremony?" Edmond says confused. "I didn't think she was all that excited about it actually."

"Her birthday," Maria and Joanna say in unison. Joanna shakes her head at Edmond. "Her birthday is the same day as the induction, did you really forget that?"

"Of course, her birthday!" Edmond laughs loudly, obviously trying to downplay his error. "Yes, we will have to do something special for her after the ceremony. In fact, I think I have a great idea."

⊕⊕⊕⊕⊕⊕⊕

Joanna shakes her head no again. *He can't really think this is a good idea.* "We will ruin her birthday with this, it's just not necessary." She walks blindly into the woods, feeling her way through the darkness.

"It's been eleven years since her Evolution Day," Edmond says, walking ahead of her. "You have never agreed to let me ask him for the answer. Why is it so easy for you to accept that she isn't truly-"

"Truly what?" Joanna hisses at him. She stops walking behind him, waiting for him to turn around and face her. "She isn't truly what, Edmond?"

He turns around but she can only make out his moonlit silhouette, his face is a blank slate. "She isn't a wolf, Joanna, and I want to know why."

"What makes you think he will know?"

"Because he always knows."

They walk in silence for a few moments. "What will having this information change for her?" Joanna finally says. "Maybe it skipped a generation like the elders said, it doesn't have to mean anything."

"She is a Dusabe, why do you desire her to be average?" Edmond argues back, not turning around. "Tessa is our only child and will carry on my—our—legacy. I need to know why she did not transition."

Joanna bites her lips nervously. *What if he really does know the reason, will Edmond ever forgive me?* They walk a little further into the woods, trees around them become denser and thicker. The buzzing sound of mosquitoes and other insects fills their ears, Joanna swats several of them away with her hands. "How much longer before we get there?" she says irritated.

"Do you remember where exactly his tree is?" Edmond grunts moodily back in response.

Great, we're probably lost.

A few steps later they walk out of the woods and into a pasture filled with a few trees. They walk up to each tree and check its trunk.

"There," Edmond says, pointing at a tall tree towards the end of the pasture, "I see it." He walks over to the tree and clears away some brush, revealing three neatly carved flag poles, directly parallel to three wavy lines above a crudely shaped opal.

Joanna nods at the markings. "We won't be able to enter his lair with clothing; the tree won't accept anything human," she says. They strip off all of their clothing and hang them on the branches of the tree. "My dialect is a little off and this will be hard to do once we transform."

Edmond nods in understanding. He rolls his shoulders, slowly growing a thick coat of dark brown fur around his entire body. Joanna lets out a slow guttural growl and grows fine, light brown hair all over her body. Their feet turn into giant paws, twice the size of a regular animal. Their faces mutate into furry muzzles with extended jaws, their teeth grow several inches, becoming blade-sharp. A bright yellow glow glazes over their pupils, completing their transformation.

EDMOND

He stands near the tree, looking at Joanna to say the words. She curls her snout, clearly uncomfortable. *Shit. We can't speak once we shift, maybe it will be different with the ancient language.*

Joanna struggles to make her mouth form words, her tongue and teeth fighting her at every turn. After a few failed attempts, she barks in frustration. Edmond grabs her shoulders, pressing them down, signaling her to relax. He rubs her jaw roughly with his paws, then moves them down to her chest, they both take a deep breath. *Calm down, you'll get it.*

Joanna opens her jaw wide, grunting the words at first. She keeps grunting until her tone changes and the short bursts of words make sense. Her voice becomes raspy from the effort, but she doesn't give up. Finally, her snout obeys.

ƛ/PΔϬ YΨᴛB†ω /PTƷ ϚZΓ†σ⊥H *(First of our kind, we ask for safe passage)*

The tree comes alive with a jolt, shaking its branches vigorously and emitting a low vibrational hum. The carved symbols on the tree begin to glow in sync with the hum. There's a sudden gust of wind as the highest branch swoops down beside them, engulfing them in an awkward hug.

I hate this part.

More branches form around them, maneuvering under their feet until they are completely trapped. The soil beneath them slowly opens until a small circle is formed, and the tree drags them underground. Small pebbles and sticks fly past their faces, leaving them both gasping for breath as they're pulled deeper into the earth. After a few moments, the tree releases them from its branches onto a cave floor. Joanna coughs up the dirt and debris from her mouth. Edmond prowls around the cave, snapping out a few aggressive barks. Joanna taps him on his shoulder. Shaking her head, she puts her paw to her mouth, and Edmond nods.

How do we find him?

Joanna leans her head back looking at the roof of the cave, it's now sealed shut. She moves her mouth to speak again, this time it only takes a few tries.

ᎬᏏᎯᏇ ᏉᎦᏒᎨᎻᏉ (*Reveal yourself, master*)

Joanna repeats the phrase five times. The cave is quiet at first then they both hear it, the subtle sounds of a web being weaved. The constant spinning and turning of silk whispers just above them. Suspending himself carefully down the cave is the first shapeshifter of Opal Island, an enormous spider known as Nanzi.

ധψ῭ρ (Here I am)

Edmond looks at Joanna confused, she moves her mouth to try and say something in the ancient language, but Nanzi pierces into their minds simultaneously.

"Why have you summoned me?" he asks them.

"I am Dusabe," Edmond responds internally to Nanzi. *"I will be the next leader of Parish One. I am here for your blessing, as is tradition."*

"Another Dusabe," Nanzi examines Edmond closely. *"You look like your father. I remember you."*

"Like my father, I need your knowledge. I want to lead for many years." Edmond answers confidently.

"We will see," Nanzi says coyly. He turns to Joanna, *"why are you here?"*

Joanna stares back at the spider dumbfounded. Edmond can tell from her stiff posture that she's intimidated by the ancestor. *I don't think she's ever been this close to him before.*

"She is here for our daughter," Edmond answers for her. *"She wants to know why she didn't turn on her Evolution Day."* Joanna turns her head sharply toward Edmond and growls. He ignores her and waits for Nanzi to respond.

She might not care, but I need to know.

Nanzi's mouth turns upwards into a horrifying smile. He looks from Edmond to Joanna and back again. *"She knows why,"* Nanzi says plainly and turns back to Joanna. *"Your plea was heard."*

Edmond looks at Joanna who is cowering her head. Before he can confront her, Nanzi begins the process of blessing Edmond.

"For my knowledge, what is my offering?" Nanzi asks.

Edmond steps towards him, presenting his forearm. *"This is our offering,"* he yelps loudly, tearing deeply into his own flesh. Biting off a small piece of his forearm, he spits it out at Nanzi's front leg.

Nanzi accepts the flesh, using one of his legs he throws it up into the large web at the top of the cave. He weaves out more strands of silk, creating a circular web directly in front of Edmond. The web spins in a counterclockwise motion, picking up speed with every rotation. Nanzi stares deeply into its center, watching Edmond seemingly blend with the web. Several dozen versions of Edmond appear as small pinpoints across the spinning web. Nanzi looks at each one of them and reads.

"The solution to your problems is within the barrier. Do not trust her. A decision, between kin or country. The wrong choice leads only to chaos." Nanzi looks up from the web and stares at Joanna. *"Your intentions must be lifted, if Contessa does not turn on her next natal day, all of Opal Island will be lost."*

He snaps out of the trance and the web disappears.

"What intentions need to be lifted?" Edmond demands. *"How do we get her to turn?"*

"It's in the Imbali," Nanzi says. Before Edmond or Joanna can respond, they feel themselves being pulled up off the ground and dragged back through the earth. Within seconds, they're deposited into the same spot in front of the tree. Edmond transforms back into a human, ripping his clothes off the branches angrily. Joanna gets dressed next to him, saying nothing.

Her intentions need to be lifted? Edmond replays Nanzi's words over and over in his mind. *She did this, Tessa is different because of her.*

"I can explain," Joanna says. "I didn't think it would work, I was just so upset..."

"Tessa deserves to hear this as well," Edmond says, cutting her off. "I'm calling Seven, we need the Imbali."

"You have to understand, I just wanted life to be better for her-I wanted her to be free from this."

"Free from our family? Our legacy?" Edmond says, barely containing his rage. "You disappoint me, Joanna. Why did I have to find out like this how ashamed you are of our people?"

"I'm not ashamed!" Joanna yells back at him. "I *only* wanted more for her."

What more could you ask for?

Edmond turns on his heel and walks back towards the Dusabe mansion, the silence between them thick with tension. He pulls out his mobile device to call Seven. "We need you at the house right away and bring the Imbali, Tessa is going to turn."

CONTESSA

Tessa hears a knock on her bedroom door. When she opens it, her parents are standing in front of her. The look on her father's face concerns her immediately.

"What's wrong?" she asks, letting them into her bedroom. Edmond sits on the edge of her bed, while Joanna stands in front of them.

"We have something we need to share with you. This is...difficult to say." Edmond rubs his hands together nervously, looking pensive. "We found out this evening why you haven't turned."

Tessa looks back and forth between her parents. "What do you mean? Who told you this information? What did they say?"

"We were told by our oldest ancestor, his name is Nanzi. He was the first shapeshifter on Opal Island. It is tradition for the future leader of the Parish to receive a prophecy, you were part of it." Edmond looks at Joanna through narrow eyes. "Your mother will explain the rest."

Joanna shifts her weight from one foot to the next looking uncomfortable. "I didn't know I was the cause," she says stiffly. "It was just words, I didn't think they would mean anything."

Just words? What is she talking about? Tessa folds her arms over her chest tightly. "Tell me, why didn't I turn?"

Joanna takes a deep breath. "When I became pregnant with you, it was unexpected. Your father and I had plans to leave Opal Island and start a new life on the mainland. We wanted a fresh start."

Edmond opens his mouth to say something then stops, clenching his jaw tightly. Joanna continues. "At the time, I felt–trapped," she says honestly. "I wasn't ready to be a parent and I felt like if you stayed here in Parish One, you would come to feel the same way I did, you would be limited to the rules of a pack, and be placed on this pedestal because you were a Dusabe. I didn't want that for you." Joanna wipes tears out of the corner of her eyes, holding her composure. "A week before you were born I said a prayer over you."

"*Master Creator, please hear me. Protect my child, and give her the strength she will need to face the unseen and the everyday evils of life. Disappointment, regret, loneliness. Give her the tools that I cannot provide, the wisdom to navigate this world. Let her be resilient, outspoken. Give her only the very best. My baby girl, I know you can hear me and feel me, I'm so sorry. I wish I could have been stronger for you. You deserve to see the world, not to be trapped here. I want so much more for you, something of your own choosing.*"

Joanna opens her eyes and looks at Tessa after reciting the prayer word for word. "I didn't know that it would have this effect. I didn't know, I'm sorry." She moves to hug her daughter but Tessa pulls away, walking towards her window.

I was supposed to be one of them, this whole time I wasn't different, I was supposed to turn.

Tessa looks at her father, his jaw is still clenched tightly. He refuses to look at Joanna.

He didn't know either.

"You thought making me an outcast would be better for me than being what I truly am?" Tessa asks bitterly. "Why did you assume I didn't want this? Why did you think being different would make me better?" she demands.

"I didn't know it would work, I didn't know this would happen," Joanna tries to defend herself.

Tessa feels hot anger surging through her body, her emotions becoming a blur. "You always think you know what's best for me, but you never gave me the chance to decide, you didn't give me a choice!" She rubs the corners of her eyes, willing her body not to cry. She walks back to the bed, standing in front of her father. "How do I turn? What do I need to do?" she says, her voice firm and determined. "I want to turn."

Edmond smiles at her brightly and gives her a big hug. "You will, Tessa. Your uncle is on his way over now with the answer. You will finally be one of us."

Tessa hugs her father back tightly, ignoring the sting she feels from his words. *He'll accept me now, he'll finally see me as a Dusabe.*

⊕⊕⊕⊕⊕⊕⊕⊕

"You underestimated your own power," Seven says to Joanna. They are sitting in the kitchen together going over what happened. Edmond is in the upstairs study on the phone while Tessa sits across from them, going through the pages of the Imbali.

"Is this the book of our history and magic?" Tessa asks, not looking up from the pages. Her eyes roam the pages with awe. "It has so much information about our history, but I also see things that look like spells and incantations."

Seven takes the book out of her hands and flips it around to face him. "That's correct. It was given to me by my grandfather and his father gave it to him. It holds everything we know about our magic and how we came to be on Opal Island."

"It doesn't say anything about Parish Two," Tessa says. "Do they have magic as well? All they taught us in school is they attacked us and we fled to this side of the island," she looks at her mother with an annoyed look. "Was all of that a lie as well?"

"Respect your mother," Seven scolds. "I know you're upset about all of this, but this is not what any of us were expecting." He sighs and speaks softly, "we all just want you to be happy, Tessa."

"Tell me the whole truth," she snips. "That will make me happy. Why did they attack us?"

"To put it simply, a difference of opinion," Seven says, choosing his words carefully. "At first they didn't care that we were shapeshifters, or that we had magic and they didn't. They were happy to share the island with us. Your grandfather was actually good friends with one of their leaders."

"It didn't matter though," Joanna interrupts him. "The more powerful we became, the more we expanded as a people, the more they started to hate us. They attacked us one night out of the blue, burned down our entire community, slaughtered hundreds of us," Joanna clenches her fists together tightly, reliving the memory. "They killed my entire family... my parents, my sisters, my brother. I barely escaped."

Tessa fiddles with the hem of her nightshirt, and a sense of shame and guilt passes through her. "I'm sorry, I didn't know. You never talk about the past, none of you do."

"And for a good reason," Edmond says, suddenly appearing in the kitchen door frame. "We didn't want to expose you to this until after your Evolution Day. There's more to being a shapeshifter than just being an animal, it comes with an understanding of our legacy, of what we fought to protect."

"You could have at least told me more about the island," Tessa grumbles under her breath. "After you fled, is that when Granddad became a leader?" she asks, already suspecting the answer to her question.

"Correct," Seven says, smiling proudly. "Your grandfather led us to this part of the island and formed the council, with the strongest werewolves that we had. He was eventually elected leader not long after you were born."

"Why did it take so long for you to take his place, dad?" Tessa asks her father pointedly. "Granddad died years ago, shouldn't you have been the leader then?"

Edmond smirks at Tessa. "Perceptive observation, Tessa. I didn't become the leader because the council decided I was not fit to lead, even though it was your grandfather's last wish that I take over Parish One. They have blocked me at every turn, but not this time. The people of the parish have spoken, now here we are."

Edmond walks over to the table and takes the Imbali in his hands. "Soon you will be able to know what it's like to be a real Dusabe and our legacy will continue." He turns to Seven, "Have you figured out how to release the intentions off of her so she can transition? Nanzi was clear she must turn on her next natal day."

Seven takes the book from his hands and frowns. "I have found the solution but it all must happen at once. The incantation must to be said right before she gets ready to turn, it's when her body will be most pliant and accepting of the spell."

Edmond nods. "We will do this after the ceremony, before midnight so it's still within her natal day." He turns towards Joanna, looking at her coldly. "She will finally be where she belongs."

Joanna's jaw ticks.

Tessa notices the exchange but says nothing.

Chelsea is never going to believe this.

RENE

Rene straightens out her skirt, waving the representative from Nessus over from the security entrance. "You made it," she smiles at him. "Welcome to Parish Two, Mr. Winter. I'm Rene." They shake hands firmly.

Mr. Winter looks around, clearly unimpressed. "Your airport security is extensive, for such a...small location. Why?"

"Don't let our modest surroundings mislead you, we have a lot to offer here. Once you get a tour of the land, you'll see why investing here will be the smartest choice."

"Any reason I had to come here this late at night?" he says, picking his overnight bag up from the floor. "Very unusual for a presentation."

"Everything will make sense when we get to our headquarters," Rene says, guiding Mr. Winter to her car. He pulls a box out of his bag and then gives it to the driver. A few moments later they drive into Parish Two.

Mr. Winter gives Rene the box. "Here's a gift from our company," he says dryly. "Our newest model of the portable EJot."

"Thank you so much," Rene says kindly. "My daughter will love this." Mr. Winter doesn't respond. They ride to the middle of the parish where her office building is located. Rene points out some of the famous landmarks, trying her best to impress him. "Over there was the battle that created the great barrier," she explains. "Opal Island was once united, but former citizens became unruly and murdered dozens of our people. Fortunately, we won that brutal fight and a barrier was created to block them from entering our land."

A little white lie, but he won't know the difference anyway.

"That barrier will be coming down soon, expanding the parish's reach and capacity," Rene says proudly. "I'll talk more about that later." She turns to the other side of the street. "As you know, we were able to rebuild because of help from the mainland. Since then, several of the businesses here were funded by mainland investors and we sell their products exclusively. We have two more openings next month, hopefully, yours will follow as a close third." She glances at him for a reaction, but his face is blank.

Give me something, you stoic jackass.

They drive up to a glass building with over twenty floors.

"Let's go up to our boardroom and discuss our proposal," Rene says as she leads them into the building, passing a solid oak front desk into an opulent glass elevator. She presses the 25th floor and it opens into a large office space, with a few employees clacking away on Nessus computers.

"You're already using our computers?" Mr. Winter remarks, entering the conference room in the middle office space. "Why do you need to expand if you're already using most of our products?"

Rene closes the door, lifting her eyebrow. *So he was listening.* She pulls a bound document from the filing cabinet in the corner and gestures for him to sit at the large glass table across from her. "It's all right here," she says, handing it to him. "We use a few here and in other places in the parish, but we want every business and home outfitted with a Nessus. Your systems combined with our new technology will ensure a growth in your profits tenfold."

Mr. Winter flips through the proposal, stopping a few times to read over the projected numbers.

"What are your thoughts?" Rene asks.

"These are some wildly ambitious promises, Ms. Kwadio," Mr. Winter stops on a certain page and scoffs. "A technology so powerful it will enhance our operating systems by 200 percent?" he reads out loud. "An average increase in our bottom line by over 120 percent year over year. What you're suggesting is alien-level technology and frankly, I don't believe it."

"I wouldn't have brought you over here if I didn't think we had something to show for it," Rene says tightly. "Would you like a demonstration?"

"Absolutely," Mr. Winter says, leaning over the desk eagerly. "Show me how this would work."

Rene presses a small button under the table.

"Yes, Ms. Kwadio," the receptionist's voice echoes through the room.

"Please let Michael know we need a demo in the main conference room."

"Right away, Ms. Kwadio," the receptionist responds.

A few minutes later a slender man with sunken dark eyes walks into the room. He's wearing a wrinkled white lab coat over a pair of khaki pants and a plaid shirt. Several sets of keys jingle from one of his belt loops. "Rene, we weren't expecting a demo today," Michael says. "Which one are we using for a test subject?"

"Cygnus," Rene says smiling, "it should be right over us in a few minutes."

"Very well," Michael says reluctantly. He walks out into the hallway and rolls a cart into the conference room. A Nessus mini laptop, a USB drive, and an oblong object lay on the top.

"This is the 'Gamma Ray'," Rene says proudly. "She's made of materials from your company as well as particles we chiseled off the barrier. This will be the third time we've tested her."

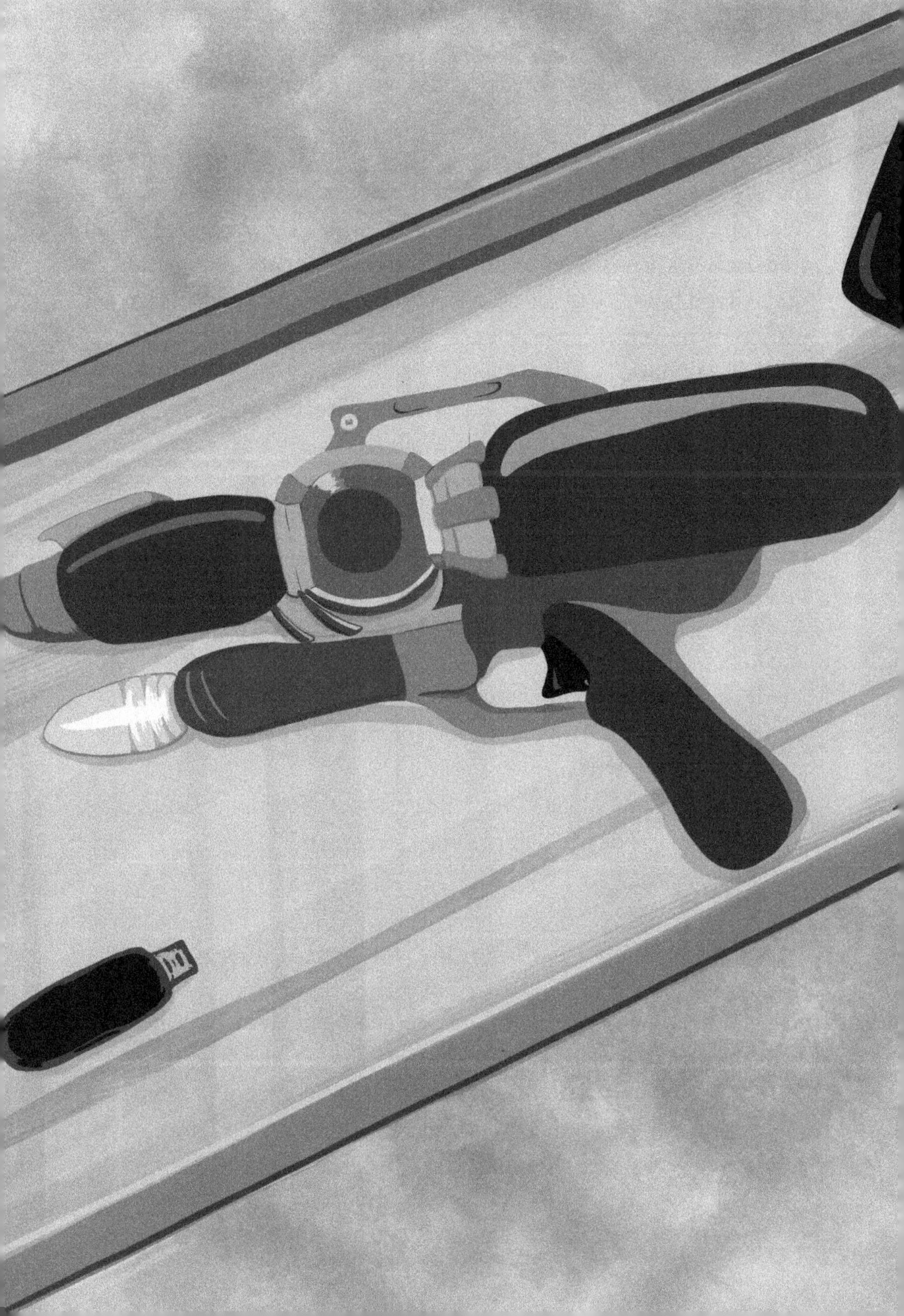

"How does it work?" Mr. Winter asks, circling the equipment cart.

Rene looks over at Michael, "I'll let our head engineer explain."

Michael pushes the cart over to the windows. He pulls one of his keys away from his belt loop and unlocks one of the windows. A strong chilly wind rushes into the room. "Gamma Ray is a translator," Michael says loudly over the wind. "At first we didn't understand how to use her power but after testing her during some planetary movement, we're sure it's just a simple conversation she's able to have."

"What does that mean?" Mr. Winter screams over the wind. "What is she talking to?"

Micheal doesn't respond. He pops the Nessus computer open and begins typing in some coordinates. "Looks like two minutes," he mumbles to himself. Michael aims Gamma Ray out the window, he moves the end of the device up and down until finally leaving it at a 45-degree angle. "Thirty-five seconds," he yells at Mr. Winter and Rene.

Mr. Winter inches closer to the device, Rene stops him before he gets right next to it. "Give it a little room, it can be...unpredictable at times," Rene warns him.

"What does that mean?" Mr. Winter says stubbornly. A loud snap goes off from the device before Rene can respond.

It's happening.

A single focused beam shoots out of Gamma Ray towards the sky. Rene runs towards a nearby window.

"This is my favorite part," she screams out in awe, "when it brings the particles alive!"

Mr. Winter comes to stand next to her. They both watch in silence as the beam connects with four points in the sky, the points connect with each other to form the outline of a large bird.

"Is that a swan?" Mr. Winter says in disbelief. "How is it possible?"

"As Michael said, it's a conversation," Rene answers, not taking her eyes off the sky. "Whatever is in the barrier, has universal matter inside it. When you focus the matter towards the sky during a cosmic event, they speak to each other somehow."

"What do you mean by a cosmic event?" Mr. Winter asks, inching closer to the window to get a better look.

"It really could mean any number of things," Michael answers quickly. "When another planet is in close orbit to ours, when the moon is in a certain position, or like tonight," he points at the sky, smiling. "Cygnus is a constellation that passes over our Parish a few times a year," Michael presses a few more keys on the computer, and the beam changes from a bright blue to a light purple hue. "Once they connect, Gamma Ray becomes the perfect extraction tool," he hits a small button and then inserts the USB drive into the device. The light purple beam slowly retracts back into Gamma Ray. Just before the last of the beam re-enters the device it hits a stray bird in the sky. The bird squawks loudly in protest and alters its course, going back towards the barrier and into Parish One.

"Once the elements are safely contained, you can harness the power," Michael says, closing the window shut. He pulls the USB from its socket, it's glowing the same shade of purple as the beam. He inserts the drive into the computer. The computer leaps a few inches off the cart, jolted awake by the powerful technology.

"Have you done this before?" Mr. Winter asks nervously. "It doesn't look like the computer likes it very much."

"We haven't," Michael says, watching the computer closely. "But our tests indicate this should work, it should pair."

The purple light from the USB slowly engulfs the computer, creating a loud buzzing sound for a few seconds then it goes black, and sits completely still.

"Gamma, acknowledge," Michael says loudly to the computer.

"Acknowledge," the computer says back to him.

"Impossible!" Mr. Winter says loudly. He moves closer to the computer, inspecting it closely. "This isn't a trick, is it? The computer is now..."

"Alive?" Rene says with a beaming smile. "Imagine every device and appliance you have, possessing true cognitive ability, doing anything you ask it to do. Imagine the possibilities."

"Email my team," Mr. Winter says wildly. "Gamma?"

"It won't work for you," Michael says, chuckling. "This computer has been modified to only respond to my voice and my fingerprints."

"Every device can only be activated by its owner, making Nessus the first company to develop a fully functional personalized computer, only responsive to the owner's commands." Rene picks up the proposal from the table and hands it to Mr. Winter. "Still think my numbers are too ambitious?"

Mr. Winter grins, taking the proposal in his hands. "How soon can we start production?"

⇔⇔⇔⇔⇔⇔⇔⇔

Rene calls an impromptu board meeting the next afternoon. The four members who stayed after her grandfather died, trickle into the conference room. Once the last member takes his seat, Rene gets straight to the point. "I know a lot of you doubt my ability to lead," she looks each of them in the eye. "Many changes have been implemented since my grandfather died, securing several businesses from the mainland to expand our economy. I called this meeting so we can celebrate another successful partnership," Rene pauses, drumming her fingertips on the glass table. The incessant beat rattles the surface. "Nessus has agreed to partner with us, the contract will be worth over $15 million in Walahadli money."

The board members look at her dumbfounded.

"But, we don't have much of the particles left," one of them says. "How are we to mass produce them, we don't have nearly enough material."

Rene flashes a mischievous glance. "It's time to take down the barrier," she says simply. "Once it's gone we'll have all the material we need."

"What about Parish One?" says another board member. "What do we do about them, about–what they are?"

"Easy," Rene says, standing up. "We *take* what we want from them. My grandfather was scared of who they used to be, but we have no idea who they are today. I say it's time we find out."

"How?" asks one of the elder board members. "We haven't made contact with them in years."

"Don't worry, I'll handle that," Rene responds breezily. "I plan on inviting them all to Vilë."

The board members try their best to disguise their shock and disgust, but they know better than to question her decisions.

"That is all gentleman, I will be in touch when I have an update." Rene looks each of them in their eyes, making sure they see the clear intent in hers. "Speak of this to no one."

The board members nod in agreement and clear the room quickly, murmuring amongst themselves on the way out. Rene catches the last sentence before the door shuts.

"She's either going to make us very rich or kill us all."

CONTESSA

SIX MONTHS EARLIER

"We're both going for captain. I don't think this is going to turn out well," Tessa says to Chelsea. "She already doesn't like me for whatever reason."

"I really think you're making this out to be more than what it is, Tess," Chelsea says, tying up her shoelaces. "She's just super competitive, don't take it personally." She puts the final touches on her double knot and starts stretching her legs.

"So I'm supposed to let her treat me like trash?" Tessa hisses back at her.

"Are you two done whispering in the corner?" Coach Yearwood barks at them. "Get in position for laps," she blows her whistle loudly. "Ten!"

Tessa and Chelsea join the rest of their netball team in laps up and down the court. Tessa looks around the open-air multi-sport complex, taking in the pace of each of her teammates. *We aren't strong enough yet.* She does two more laps keeping an eye on the weaker links. On her third lap, she can see the sun rays catching up to most of the group.

By lap eight, everyone struggles to get up and down the court in the broiling heat, except Tessa and Margaret.

"Very good, guys." Coach Yearwood claps and points at them. "Take notes, this is captain material."

Margaret speeds up a little to get in front of Tessa. "Are you getting tired, princess?" she mocks her.

"Not even a little," Tessa lies. A sharp pain shoots up her side as she tries to control her breathing. *Don't quit, Tess. Keep pushing, keep pushing.*

They are neck and neck at the line for the last lap. Tessa keels over in pain as the rest of their team trickle in behind them.

"Damn, you girls are fast." Chelsea wheezes, collapsing on the ground next to them.

"Enjoy that rest, we're back in ten minutes to start running drills," Coach Yearwood yells at the team. She takes out a mesh net filled with netballs and throws them around the court. "I want three people per ball." She motions towards the center circle. "Practice defense here, wing attack, and wing defense in the other two corners." Coach Yearwood motions for Tessa and Margaret to meet her in the goal defense circle. "I know you both want this, so I'm making my decision for team captain today."

Great. I was not prepared for this at all. Tessa looks over at Margaret quickly, she flashes her a condescending smile. *I can't let her beat me.* She takes a deep breath, centering all of her energy on the task at hand. *Just get through it, prove that you're better than her.*

"What do we have to do?" Margaret asks the coach gleefully.

"Defend your goal and be a captain at the same time. I need to know what kind of leaders you girls are," she blows her whistle in three quick bursts. "We're going to do one drill over and over again," she passes out numbered jerseys to each girl. "Odds vs evens. Tessa, you're defending this goal, Margaret is trying to get through you. We do this until I say stop." Coach Yearwood jogs over to the sidelines. "Begin!"

The team runs the drill for a few moments, stopping several times to take direction from Coach Yearwood. She places feet, positions hands, and calls out fouls. "If this is how we're going to play against the Parish champions we might as well just give up, we've lost!" she screams from the sidelines. "Is this how you plan to defend, Janet? You back down every single time someone advances. Step into that charge and don't let anyone get past you!"

Margaret and Tessa are left in the goal defense circle, waiting on Coach Yearwood to be satisfied enough for them to play a full drill.

"I bet you think you can take this like you take everything else," Margaret says suddenly. "Like you've earned this in some way just because your family runs this place."

"What the hell are you talking about?" Tessa snaps. "I'm working hard to get this, just like you."

"You're nothing like me," Margaret shoots back. "All that power in your last name but none of it in your blood, you're not even a wolf."

Tessa stands up tall from her squat position. "What did you just say?"

"I forget your ears aren't as good because you don't have *our* senses," Margaret says, turning to face her. "I said, you're not a real wolf and don't deserve to be captain of anything."

Tessa grinds her teeth, seething with anger. "You're not better than me," she says, getting back into her defensive stance. "Watch." Tessa takes two quick steps to her left, catching an incoming ball and throwing it back out to the team.

"Are you two having a tea party or playing?" Coach Yearwood yells in their direction. "Pay attention, Margaret. Defend your goal!"

"I hope you enjoyed that," Margaret says, turning around to look intensely at the court. "That was the last one."

The next ball comes sailing into the goal defense, Tessa tries to block it again but Margaret intercepts her block and throws it back out to the wing defense player. They catch it and throw it again, this time making it into the net. The team yells in joy, as Margaret looks back at Tessa with a determined look on her face. The drills continue like this for another hour, Tessa and Margaret fighting every inch of the way. Coach Yearwood blows her whistle.

"This is the kind of hustle we need against the reigning Saint Piggotts! If we're going to meet them at the last game we have to push ourselves, be willing to work twice as hard," she says beaming at her team. "Ok, the score is tied up, and this is the last goal. Let's see if you can make it. Everyone, get back to position–and go!"

The whistle shrieks and Tessa bends down into position, the ball comes her way but instead of catching it, she lets Margaret grab it and throw it back out. When her team member goes to shoot the ball again, Tessa sidesteps Margaret quickly and dives in front of the ball. She's less than a centimeter away from grabbing it when Margaret grabs at her, digging sharp nails into her shoulder. Tessa misses the interception, and the ball goes effortlessly into the hoop. She grabs at her shoulder in pain. *She turned! That's forbidden unless we're fighting an enemy.* Tessa grabs the back of Margaret's jersey, pulling her to the ground next to her.

"You cheater! You turned!" Tessa yells.

Margaret scratches at her wildly. "You're not one of us," she yells loudly. "You will never be one of us!"

"Hey, hey, hey!" Coach Yearwood yells, she runs over to the girls and separates them. "Stop it you two, stop! What's the issue?"

"She turned!" Tessa yells, getting herself off the floor. "She scratched at me and I missed the interception."

"I did not," Margaret says innocently. "Tessa is just upset she missed and wants to blame it on someone, I know the rules."

"Did anyone see this?" Coach Yearwood looks around at the team. Everyone shakes their head no. "Tessa, attacking your teammate is not ok," the coach begins to lecture.

"She attacked me! Look," she shows the coach her shoulder. Coach Yearwood inspects Tessa's arm. The scratches look more like welts than deep cuts.

"She got those because she *missed* the ball and fell to the ground on her shoulder," Margaret says. "I don't need to fight for something that I'm already better at. Stop making excuses and admit you lost."

Tessa goes to say something but Coach Yearwood blows her whistle. "Showers, now everyone."

Tessa starts to walk off but Coach Yearwood holds her back. "I need to talk to the two of you privately." The three of them walk into the small office at the back of the court. The coach turns to face both of them after Tessa closes the door. "Margaret, be honest with me, did you turn, did you hurt her?"

"I swear coach I didn't!" Margaret says earnestly.

"She's a liar! I'm telling you-" Tessa begins.

"Save it." Coach Yearwood says sternly. "Tessa, I'm not saying either of you is wrong here, but with no other witnesses or proof I have to let this go."

Tessa shakes her head and folds her arms. *This is absolute bullshit.*

"As for team captain, I feel like both of you would make excellent leaders, but Margaret showed real heart out there today, she went above and beyond to defend and attack, all things I need in a captain."

"Thank you, coach, I promise you I won't let you down!" Margaret gushes.

Tessa rubs her shoulder angrily. *She will only bring the team down-I can't be the only one who sees that.*

"I really hope not, Margaret. We need that kind of fight if we're going to make it to the championships," Coach Yearwood says, slowly turning to Tessa. "I'd really like it if you were co-captain, I think with some time and development-"

"No thanks," Tessa says quickly. "You know what coach? I think the team would actually be better off without me."

"Don't be ridiculous! You're a great player and the games start next week, we need you to make it through the final rounds," the coach pleads.

Margaret raises her eyebrows, surprised at the Coach's accolades.

I'm never going to be at peace, she's going to make my life hell.

"No, I think it's best I sit this one out, you can use my sub for the games. I'm sorry."

Before the coach can respond, Tessa walks out of the office.

A week later, the entire team stopped speaking to Tessa, except Chelsea.

⊄⊅⊄⊅⊄⊅⊄⊅

PRESENT-DAY

Tessa hears the roar of the complex as she gets out of the car. Crowds of people are lined outside, waiting to see who becomes the Parish Netball High School Champion. A whistle goes off and a loud moan from the crowd pierces the air.

"What kind of call was that!" someone screams over the crowd.

Tessa hesitates a little, keeping one foot firmly planted in the vehicle.

"Everything ok, Ms. Tessa?" Taino, the family driver, looks back at her with concern. "I can come in with you, or get one of your father's security to come and escort you in."

"No, that's ok," Tessa says, smiling back at him. "I just didn't expect this many people to be here."

"You sure you feel okay to go in alone? I can call some security guards," Taino says again.

"You wouldn't ask my mother if she needed security," Tessa says, a little snappier than she meant.

"Yes, but your mother is different," Taino says matter-of-factly.

Yes, she's a wolf, she can defend herself.

"It's fine," Tessa closes the door and waves him away. *Soon I won't need security ever again.*

Tessa walks into the complex, ignoring the looks of various citizens of Parish One. An older man walking towards her stops suddenly and stares her down.

"Is that you, young Dusabe?" the man asks her kindly. "I haven't seen you around in a while, how's your father?"

"He's doing well," Tessa says in a rehearsed tone. "Very excited about his induction on Saturday."

"Aren't we all," the man says dryly. "Another wolf trying to lead us off a cliff." The man hobbles away shaking his head. A few people behind them notice who she is and start whispering to themselves. Tessa takes a deep breath and tries her best to ignore it.

People will always have an opinion. Let it go.

The cheers from the crowd get louder and louder as she walks toward the entrance of the court. She checks the scoreboard quickly to see her old team in the lead by five points with less than ten minutes left in the game. She scans the players until she spots Chelsea, playing hard defense by the goal line.

"LET'S GO, CHELSEA!" Tessa screams from the top of her lungs. Chelsea looks around confused, then she spots Tessa and flashes a huge grin.

Moments later the opposing team, Saint Piggotts, scores a goal getting several boos from the crowd. To her left, Tessa can hear the popular radio host Viper doing his radio broadcast in a small glass booth above the stands.

His voice booms out of the speakers.

"The Saint Piggotts' players are showing no mercy to their rivals this evening. The Elsyk players will have to make a comeback or keep them at bay for another seven minutes now with a one-point lead. Coach Yearwood, looking tense in her corner of the court, throws out plays. This would be the first championship for the all-girls private school, Elsyk. Let's see what they can produce."

Tessa looks over at Coach Yearwood, she's scribbling furiously into a notebook, her forehead has a deep crease in the middle. A few paces away from Coach Yearwood is Margaret, she's talking to one Janet while pointing at the court. She jabs Janet in the chest, getting closer to her face. Tessa looks away, shoving down her anger. *I should have been captain. I should be leading us in this game, not that bully.* She refocuses her attention on the game, keeping her eyes on the clock. *Four more minutes and we have the ball. They can pull this off.* A girl whose name she can't remember goes for a pass but gets blocked in by the defense. Coach Yearwood screams at her from the sidelines to pass the ball. The girl looks around but nobody is free. "SHOOT IT!" Tessa yells impulsively. "SHOOT THE BALL!" The player takes a step back and aims her hands at the goal just as the clock hits two minutes. She makes a wild throw and misses but one of her teammates snatches the ball before it hits the ground and throws the ball at the goal again.

This time it's good.

The crowd gets to their feet, stomping and screaming, ALMOST THERE! ALMOST THERE! Saint Piggotts calls a time-out with 45 seconds left. Tessa can feel the excitement bubbling around her as the players take their positions on the court. Her adrenaline feels tapped into the crowd's energy like they're all humming the same song. Seconds tick by slowly while the Saint Piggotts players scramble to make a goal. One of their players shoots down the court but misses the shot, a few seconds later the buzzer goes off and the game is over. A cacophony of cheers pours over the complex. Everyone is up in their seats, clapping and yelling loudly. Tessa watches in envy as Margaret gets lifted up in the air by the rest of the team while Coach Yearwood looks on, clearly fighting back her emotions.

Things will be different soon. I will finally be accepted.

❖❖❖❖❖❖❖❖

"I can't believe her prayer worked though," Chelsea says, rubbing her temples with her hands. "To completely stop your transformation merely from her intentions, that's some powerful stuff."

"Yeah, but it's not what I wanted," Tessa replies. "She made that choice for me when I wasn't even born yet, that doesn't seem right." She takes another spoonful of ice cream into her mouth, making sure not to drip anything on the leather seats. "Can you drive around the market a few more times, Taino?" she asks politely. "I'm not ready to head home just yet."

"No problem, Ms.Tessa," he replies, making another circle around the market square.

Chelsea pops the last piece of her ice cream cone into her mouth, playing the shiny gold medal around her neck. "I wish you could have been part of this," she says to Tessa. "You would have been a kinder captain."

"You guys still won, so what difference does it make now," Tessa says grudgingly.

Chelsea stops admiring the medal and looks at Tessa seriously. "Now that you're going to turn, will our plans change? Do you still want to go to the mainland after the summer?"

Crap! I forgot about that.

Tessa looks up meekly from her ice cream cup. "I think that's out the window now, Chels. I'm the only child, which means I will eventually be in charge," she releases a long sigh. "Not that I'm excited about that either."

Chelsea nods in understanding. "I guess it will be a one-man band then," she frowns and looks out the window. "Maybe it's for the best, who knows what it's like there."

"I'm sorry to interrupt," Taino says, looking at Tessa in the rear-view mirror. "Are you speaking of Walahadli?"

"We are," Chelsea says eagerly. "Have you ever been?"

"When I was a younger man," Taino says, smiling to himself. "I lived there for several years. It's an exciting place for sure....so many things to do, places to see."

"Why did you come back here?" Tessa says, not hiding her confusion.

Taino furrows his brow, "I never felt at home there," he says simply. "Everything about that place feels calculated, inhumane."

Chelsea and Tessa look at each other with raised eyebrows.

I've never heard him speak like this. What happened?

Before she could ask, Chelsea's phone pings once, then twice, then four more times.

"Everyone's going to Margaret's house to celebrate," she says, reading the texts out loud. "You're more than welcome to come."

"No, I'm not," Tessa says laughing. "I know she won't want me there, and most of the team hates me for quitting." She takes the last few bites of her ice cream, hoping the cold sweetness will wash over her jealousy.

"You can drop me off at home, I'll have my mom drive me over, she's on her way back from the complex now," Chelsea says. The rest of the car ride is filled with the sounds of the radio. Viper is recapping the game and the historic victory for the Elysk girls' high school. When they get to Chelsea's house, Tessa gets out to hug her best friend quickly.

"I'm so happy for you, Chels. Congrats, you guys deserve it!"

"Thanks," Chelsea says, hugging her back. "I know it sucks right now, but in two days you will be a brand new person, this is what you always wanted, right?"

"It is, I'm just so nervous. Nobody has ever turned this late before, none of us know what to expect."

"You'll do great," Chelsea says walking towards her house. "What's the worst that could happen?"

EDMOND

S how them no fear, none. Edmond takes a few deep breaths before walking into the basement level of The Colosseum. The smell of mothballs and dust attack his nostrils immediately, he walks through a narrow, dimly lit hallway that ends at a door. When he opens the door, everyone turns to look at him. The four members of the council are to his right, dressed in their traditional robes. They are huddled in a corner, whispering to themselves. To his left are twelve wolves in human form, about half his pack, including Seven. Behind them, sulking in the corner is the wolf Edmond beat to become the leader of Opal Island, Luther. They lock eyes instantly. Luther grimaces at him and looks away. He can feel the eyes of the council members staring him down as he takes his place in the center of the room. *No fear.*

"Good evening, brethren," Edmond says to the crowd. "We are approaching a historic day in our history. Our people have voted and spoken, it's time for a Dusabe to lead this Parish into a new direction once again." Most of the pack claps loudly, Seven especially. Luther and the council remain silent. "I know my father left some large shoes to fill but it has been ten years since his passing and we're worse off than when he was alive," Edmond stares directly at the council, meeting each set of eyes with intensity. "Our semi-barter economy continues to put our citizens into debt and despair, our fields are barely producing crops and our treasury is nearly empty. A change is mandatory and critical for our survival."

"No need for another campaign speech," Luther says from the corner, his face exhibiting a threatening scowl. "What did the spider say? That is what we all want to hear. What did he tell you?"

Edmond walks over to Luther, standing just a few inches away from his face. "Who is currently speaking?" he asks him sternly.

Luther clenches his jaw and narrows his eyes, but doesn't respond.

Edmond flexes his right hand, slowly transforming his nails into sharpened claws. He grabs Luther by the neck, digging his forefinger into his flesh. "Who is speaking?" he asks again, emphasizing each word exactly.

The rest of the room watches in silence, knowing not to intervene.

"The alpha," Luther spits out at him, the hatred in his eyes blazing wildly.

Edmond lets him go and walks back to the center of the room. "We will be prosperous again, we are the strongest creatures on *either* side of this island. The people of this Parish look up to us and we will no longer fail them," he pauses to look around the room. "I have spoken with our oldest ancestor, the first shapeshifter of this land, Mjomba Buiboy Nanzi. He has confirmed to me that our problems have a simple solution. The barrier."

The room breaks out into whispers and grunts of concern. The council members look at each other with a knowing glance. They stare at Edmond with blank expressions.

"If we wish to succeed," Edmond yells over the voices in the room, "we will have to remove the barrier."

"This is a fool's errand, boy," one of the council members says from across the room. The four of them stare at Edmond with cold hard eyes. "You have no idea the repercussions this will cause."

The rest of the room murmurs in agreement. "What will happen to our families? What if they hunt us again?" Several wolves speak out at once, throwing questions at Edmond. He raises his hand and the room goes silent.

"The barrier has made the choice for us already," Edmond says knowingly. "Last week a small tunnel was discovered, it's about a half mile long and it leads directly to the other side."

"Impossible," a council member yells loudly over the muttering in the room. "The barrier has been stable for decades, there has never been a crack in it, and now there's a full tunnel?" The council members step together in unison, inching closer to Edmond. "What did you do, Dusabe?"

"I paid attention," Edmond snaps back at them angrily. "Whether you like it or not, things are about to change," he turns to look at everyone in the room. "We can't escape it now, a shift is coming."

⊕⊕⊕⊕⊕⊕⊕

"If you keep tapping your foot it will eventually fall off," Edmond says to Brooks jokingly. They are sitting in Brooks' truck, parked on a dirt road right next to the barrier.

"Are you sure this was the meeting time?" Brooks asks, checking the digital clock on his dashboard once again. The time reads 12:11am.

"I'm sure," Edmond says calmly. "We made sure it was late at night so nobody would see him, he's only ten minutes late so don't panic."

"Don't panic?" Brooks turns to Edmond with raised eyebrows. "Ed, I have been with your family since your father took power. I saw firsthand how he changed this island and how far we've come as a Parish. What you're doing could jeopardize everything he has built." He shakes his head, looking out the window. "I know I'm only a human, but even your pack is worried about this, please tell me you know what you're doing."

Edmond inhales deeply, "I've already explained this a thousand times to you," he says impatiently. "When I discovered the tunnel you were the only person I told because you're the only person I trust with my life, human or not, you have proven yourself loyal to my family for decades. I need you to trust me."

Brooks nods and he turns on the radio. Viper's voice sails smoothly through the car. "Good evening night owls, we're in the middle of our classical iktala night, next up we have Dion Salin accompanied by the Walahadl orchestra, enjoy." Music fills the old truck as Edmond and Brooks sit and wait. Half an hour goes by before Edmond gets truly concerned.

It should not be taking him this long, if something happened to him, my whole plan is lost.

He looks out the window just in time to see a small bluebird land a few inches away from the truck. Seconds later, the bird has transformed into a young boy about 14 years old. He scurries to the truck, his hands and legs freshly bruised. Edmond gets out of the truck to meet him. "What happened?" he demands, grabbing the boy by his collar. "Why did you take so long? What did you see?"

The boy wriggles out of Edmond's grasp, trying to catch his breath.

"They caught me," he says breathlessly. "I don't know how they saw me but I turned in a dark alley and when I came out, she was waiting for me." The boy shivers in fear from the memory. "She questioned me for hours. I'm sorry, Mr. Dusabe," the boy breaks down in tears, rubbing the bruises on his hands and legs. "I'm so sorry."

"What did you tell them?" Brooks asks quickly. "What do they know?"

"No," Edmond says, cutting Brooks off. "Tell me who *she* is first, is their leader a woman?"

The boy nods, wiping tears and snot from his face. "It's like she was waiting for me or something, she knew exactly where and when I landed in the Parish. I couldn't escape, I'm sorry."

Cameras, she must have the entire Parish covered with them, that's the only way.

"What did she say when she caught you, what does she want?" Edmond presses him.

The boy digs into his right pocket and retrieves a neatly folded letter.

"Here, she told me to give this to you."

Edmond takes the letter and reads it quickly.

Dear Mr. Dusabe,

    My name is Rene Kwadio and I am the President of Parish Two. I'm sure this isn't how you intended us to meet but I knew this day would come eventually. It isn't very polite to spy on your neighbors, but given our icy history, I understand your caution. Thank you for pointing out the tunnel in the wall, our surveillance does not go that far into the woods and without your little birdy, I would have never found it.

    Now that we have the formalities out of the way I have a proposition for you. Your little spy has informed me that your Parish isn't doing so well, in fact, it sounds like most of your citizens are on the verge of poverty. I think we can help solve each other's problems. In exchange for a large sum of money (to be discussed later) and connections for trade on the mainland of Walahadli, I would like to tear down the barrier. I think it's been too long since our communities broke bread and I'm ready to end this cold war between us. I never believed the stories about your people being different but having seen it for myself, I know that your power can no longer be ignored. I think we can help each other, and give both of our Parishes what they want.

    I have instructed two of my men to stand guard on our side of the tunnel, and you can leave your response with them. I eagerly await your reply.

Best wishes,

Rene Kwadio

Edmond reads the letter twice, making sure he didn't miss a thing. He refolds it and puts it in his pocket.

"Well, what did she say? Can we trust her?" Brooks asks anxiously.

Nanzi's voice rings in Edmond's ears instantly. *Do not trust her.*

He looks at the boy sternly. "What did you tell her about our Parish?"

"I, I.." the boy stammers looking down at the floor. "I had to-I'm sorry, they wouldn't stop hitting me," fresh tears spring from his eyes. "I couldn't help it."

Edmond looks at him, his face void of any sympathy or emotion. "You betrayed us," he says coldly, leaning down to face the boy at eye level. "You told her we had no money and now she has the leverage."

"He's just a kid, Ed," Brooks says evenly. "You can't blame him for this."

"But I can," Edmond says, not taking his eyes off the youngster, "and I do." Edmond wraps one hand around the boy's neck, squeezing tightly.

"Please," the boy begs, gasping for breath. "I'm sorry."

"Not good enough," Edmond says, grasping his neck tighter. "You're useless to me now."

"Wait," the boy slams both of his fists on Edmond's hand. "I have more information," he wheezes out between gasps for air.

Edmond releases his hold, dropping the boy to the ground. "Say it," Edmond barks at him loudly.

"When she captured me, I went to a large building in the middle of the city, that's where the headquarters are, I think. We passed a room that looked like a lab and I saw something."

"What did you see?" Brooks asks.

"It looked like a weapon of some kind, it had a weird glowing bulb on it," the boy chokes on his last words, trying again to catch his breath. "It looked important."

Edmond considers his words for a moment. "Looks like we got some leverage back, Brooks," he says, still deep in thought. "We have to find a way to get the weapon out of Parish Two before she can use it."

Edmond goes back to the truck and grabs a pen and paper. "If you want to make this up to me and spare your life," he says, writing on the piece of paper, "go back through the tunnel and give this to one of the guards standing on the other side." Edmond hands the boy the letter. He snatches it out of his hands and runs up the dirt road toward the barrier.

"What did you say to her?" Brooks asks nervously.

"I invited her to the induction ceremony," Edmond says coolly.

"Why would you do that?" Brooks yells at him. "We don't know what she's capable of, this is dangerous, Ed."

"I know what *I'm* capable of," Edmond looks at Brooks with a crooked smile. "This is only an introduction, I plan on taking that money from her and the weapon."

He turns towards the barrier, "then I'll kill her."

CONTESSA

"Are you sure you want to take them out?" Mrs. Pryce frowns. "It's been a tradition since you were five, are you sure?"

Tessa looks at herself in the mirror again, clipping and unclipping one of the gold clips in her hair. *Everything is about to change, why not start now?* "Yes. I'm sure. Take them out, then put my hair into this style."

She shows a picture to Mrs. Pryce.

"Ok, Tess," Mrs. Pryce works her way through Tessa's hair, unclipping each ornament carefully and placing them in a velvet bag. Each time she unfastens a clip she combs through the piece of loose hair with a special wax Joanna bought from the marketplace. "Your mom won't like this."

"Do you think the pack will accept me?" Tessa asks, ignoring her comment. "Nobody has ever turned this late before. I don't know what they will think of all this."

"Your father will make sure everyone stays in line," Mrs. Pryce says knowingly. "Don't worry about it, this is a long time coming."

Mrs. Pryce adds extra wax to a hard knot in the middle of Tessa's head. "You'll get to go to the pack meetings now as well, be part of the community."

Tessa picks up one of the gold clips and plays with it between her fingers. "What was it like when I was little? When I didn't turn," she asks. "Did people get upset?"

"Upset isn't the right word," Mrs. Pryce says quickly. "I think your parents were confused and honestly, a little embarrassed.

They made a big deal about your Evolution Day, there was a huge party. But then..."

"Nothing happened," Tessa finishes. "What did they do then?"

"Everything they could think of," Mrs. Pryce smiles to herself. "The village elder said it probably skipped a generation but your father refused to believe that. He was never satisfied with any of the answers. He knew there was something else."

"Too bad he's still disappointed," Tessa mumbles. Mrs. Pryce stops combing her hair and spins the chair around so they're facing each other.

"Your parents have only ever loved you, Contessa," she says firmly. "I have been with this family since you were born and trust me when I say, there is nothing they wouldn't do for you."

She cups Tessa's face with both her hands. "They are very proud of you."

Tessa nods her head, releasing herself from Mrs. Pryce's hands. "Let's hope I don't mess this up, my anxiety is through the roof!"

Mrs. Pryce spins the chair around a few times, making Tessa a little dizzy as she laughs hysterically. "Wait, wait, stop!" Tessa squeals on the fourth spin. "You're going to make me throw up!"

Mrs. Pryce stops the chair and continues combing Tessa's hair. "You're going to make a fine wolf, you'll see."

⊕⊕⊕⊕⊕⊕⊕⊕

I might still have time, I just need to figure out where she's sitting.

"Tessa, did you hear me?" Joanna snaps in front of her. "You need to stand next to us, stop peeking in."

"Sorry," Tessa says, stepping away from the back entrance. She walks down a few stone steps onto a cobbled pathway. Standing outside The Colosseum with her family, Tessa waits for their entrance to be announced.

"I was hoping to spot Chelsea, I need to talk to her."

"You can talk to her afterward, focus right now," Joanna says irritably. She looks at Tessa's hair and curls up her nose. "Did Mrs. Pryce do your hair? I don't like it."

"I asked her to do it," Tessa says defensively. "Things are about to change, right?"

Joanna sighs with distaste. "You could have told me, I don't think it suits you."

She turns around, walking a little closer to the entrance.

Tessa struggles to keep her anger and anxiety at bay. The sound of banging drums jolts her out of her emotions. About half a dozen procession drummers, dressed in matching silver and red outfits make their way down the cobblestone path, standing directly in front of the family. One of the drummers beats five consecutive taps, signaling everyone is ready to see the Dusabe family. Uncle Seven appears from the corner of the building, hiking up his elaborate black and gold high priest ceremonial robe as he walks so it won't drag on the floor.

"Are you ready for this?" Seven asks Edmond.

"Absolutely, brother," Edmond says proudly, showing a wide smile.

Seven smiles back at him and turns to Tessa, "and what about you soon-to-be wolf?" he grins at his niece lovingly. "Happy birthday."

"Happy birthday, my baby girl," Joanna chimes in from behind them. She consumes Tessa in a giant hug.

"Mom, stop," Tessa says lightly, pushing her away, "you're going to ruin my makeup."

"Happy birthday, Tess," Edmond says without moving. "I'm so proud of you, this evening will be the perfect birthday gift."

"Nobody has said anything about tonight," Tessa says to Seven. "What will it be like, will it hurt? What should I expect?"

Seven looks at Joanna and Edmond with a worried glance. "Honestly, I have no idea, nobody has ever changed this late in our pack before, I'm not sure how your body will react."

Great. I knew this was going to be harder than I wanted it to be.

"What does it usually feel like?" she asks her parents.

Before they can respond, the last drummer has made his way into The Colosseum hallway and the usher is signaling Seven to come forward. "We'll be there every step of the way with you, Tess," Seven says walking into the building. "For now, let's focus on getting your father inducted."

Seven and Edmond grin at each other widely before he vanishes.

"Lucky me, I get to walk down the aisle with two beautiful women by my side," Edmond says, standing in between Tessa and Joanna.

Joanna smiles, kissing him on the cheek.

The trio walks into the building passing pews filled with dozens of citizens of Parish One dressed in their finest garments. The drummers have stopped just short of the grand altar, signaling the family to move past them and walk up the three carpeted stairs to the head table where Seven is standing, holding the Imbali.

As they take their seats, the grand hall is replete with a brief silence.

Seven walks up to the microphone on the altar. "Distinguished guests and friends, we gather today to celebrate the triumph of democracy in our great nation. After a landslide victory, it's my honor to declare Edmond Dusabe, my brother, the new Prime Minister of Opal Island."

Applause erupts around The Colosseum, echoing off the marble walls. Edmond stands up and gives a little wave to the crowd, grinning widely.

Tessa locks eyes with Chelsea, who is sitting in the front row with her father, Brooks. They give each other a bemused familiar look. Edmond takes his seat and Seven continues.

"Opal Island has seen many turning points within its short history. Edmond has proven himself a capable and skilled leader, ready to move forward where our father, the first leader of this great Parish, left off. We remember him now and forever for the impact he has left on us all," Seven lights a candle next to the microphone and prays over it. When he lifts his head a large portrait of their late father is revealed in the background of the altar. "We salute you, Isaiah Dusabe."

Edmond looks at the picture with pride while Tessa looks on with indifference.

How can you know someone your entire life and not have any real memories of them? I have no idea who you really were. Tessa gets buried in her thoughts, tuning out her uncle as she scans the crowd. She feels someone watching her closely, someone she has never seen before. Tessa looks away and then looks back, but the woman is still gazing at her.

Who are you?

Tessa feels a small pinch on her arm.

"Pay attention," Joanna mouths to her quietly. Tessa sits up in her chair a little and tunes back into what her uncle is saying.

"My father founded this part of the island and created a fair and thriving economy," Seven says to the crowd. "I know my brother will carry on his legacy. Before we begin with the official swearing-in, Edmond has prepared a few words."

Tessa feels eyes lingering on her again and turns her attention back to the pews. The strange woman is looking directly at her, then at her mother, then back at her. She smiles at Tessa and Tessa smiles back, a sense of unease settles in her chest.

Who are you?

EDMOND

The crowd applauds for a full minute before Edmond can start his speech. "Thank you, thank you all so much for the applause. This reaction is humbling." He takes a deep breath, trying to steady his emotions. "Thank you to my brother Seven, and my wife and daughter for continuously teaching me how to be a good leader. I'm honored to be part of your family." He looks toward Tessa and Joanna and smiles.

"I was born and raised on this island and have been fortunate enough to see it develop and change over the years. Nothing brings me greater pride than to be a part of that change. This great nation has trusted me to lead us in a new progressive direction—I will not fail you. I'm pleased to announce that for the first time in Opal Island history, a meeting of both sides of the island is happening. Right here, today."

The woman in the crowd that was staring at Tessa stands up and walks toward the grand altar. Quiet whispers descend over the hall as she makes her way next to Edmond. He can feel the council members' eyes on him from behind the altar, the hatred searing into his back like a hot knife. *That's right, I brought her here and didn't tell you. I no longer need your permission.*

"For too long, the territories have been divided," Edmond says into the microphone, confidently. "The legacy of Opal Island must be, first and foremost, unity. The barrier also seems to agree. We have discovered a tunnel to the other parish within the barrier." The Colosseum erupts with voices. Everyone is asking several

questions at once. A few people slip out the back, shaking their heads in disgust.

I will have to get the names of those who left, that is not acceptable. Edmond raises his hands. "All of your questions will be answered in due time. For now, let me introduce the leader from beyond our borders, as we pave the way for a united Opal Island, Ms. Rene Kwadio."

The guests reluctantly clap, while looking at each other in disbelief. A few more people leave from the side of the room. Edmond tries to memorize their faces. *This is a good idea. You all don't know it yet, but this will finally bring us into the future.* Edmond takes his seat, Joanna is in his ear instantly.

"What the hell is this?" she whispers to him viciously. "Why didn't you tell me about this?"

"It's what my dad always wanted," Edmond lies smoothly. "We can talk about this later, okay?" He squeezes her hand reassuringly. "I promise, this is for the best."

Joanna puts on a fake smile and turns back toward the crowd. *This is for the best,* Edmond repeats to himself a few times, making sure none of his self-doubts reflect on his face.

"Thank you for that wonderful introduction, and congratulations on your newly appointed leadership," Rene says warmly. "This is truly a historic day for us all. I know we don't know much about each other, but I speak on behalf of all my people in Parish Two when I say, we're so excited to learn and grow together as one island. It's time to put the past behind us." She turns her head toward the main table. "I can't wait to finish what our ancestors started and move together in solidarity. Thank you again for hosting me as your honored guest and congratulations!"

Edmond stands up and embraces Rene, causing the room to go completely silent. "This change will be beneficial to everyone. We are so excited to welcome you."

"Thank you," Rene says, pulling away from the embrace. "I would also like to invite everyone to Vilë, it's an annual tradition in

Parish Two where we celebrate freedom and togetherness. Every-one is welcome!"

"A fantastic idea, our first gathering together as neighbors," Edmond helps her down the steps and then looks for his brother. "Seven, are we ready to continue?"

Seven shuffles back over to the microphone carrying the Imbali. "We're going to talk about this with the others later," he whispers to his brother. "You shouldn't have invited her."

Edmond doesn't acknowledge whether he heard the comment. Seven stands directly in front of him, holding up the thick papyrus book, its edges are torn and frayed.

"Repeat after me. I, Edmond Fanon Dusabe, solemnly swear."

"I, Edmond Fanon Dusabe, do solemnly swear."

"To uphold and represent the people of Opal Island to the best of my ability."

"To uphold and represent the people of Opal Island to the best of my ability." Edmond feels tingles going through his spine as the book responds to his words.

"I will serve dutifully and justly, putting all others before *my-self.*" Seven emphasizes the last word with a harsh tone, but Edmond doesn't flinch.

"I will serve dutifully and justly, putting all others before my-self." The cover of the Imbali starts to feel like soft, wet dough. Edmond's hand starts to sink slowly into the cover.

"I do so swear on the names of those before and after me."

"I do so swear on the names of those before and after me." Edmond's handprint gets locked into the book, binding his words to his handprint. He doesn't flinch when it takes a few drops of his blood and soaks them into the binding.

"Everyone, in reverence, we will recite the prayer." Seven sig-nals everyone to bow their heads. "Master Creator, thank you for the continued blessings over our sovereign land. We ask today that you touch the heart of this man who has been chosen to lead. We do all things through you, the Divine. Let no enemy pull us asunder. In your name, forever. UKWELI."

Edmond turns to his citizens, beaming with pride. "Everyone, over to the banquet hall. Let's eat!"

CONTESSA

While her parents are mingling with the guests, Tessa and Chelsea are talking quietly to themselves at the head table of the banquet hall.

"What do you think of this whole 'one island' pitch my dad is pushing?" Tessa asks.

"Truth?"

"Always."

"I think it's a bad idea," Chelsea says honestly. "We don't know anything about each other, we've been enemies for years. Why now?"

"Right!" Tessa agrees. "He didn't tell us anything about the tunnel or about inviting her over here. He just sprung it on all of us."

"This just keeps getting weirder and weirder. What did your mom say?"

"She looks happy, but she's furious." Tessa looks over at her mother, who is in the middle of a deep conversation with one of the guests. "She hates surprises like this."

Chelsea is about to respond but sees Rene walking over to their table smiling brightly, she nudges Tessa quickly.

"I don't believe we officially met," Rene says, coming up to the both of them. She reaches out her hand. "So nice to meet you, Contessa."

"You can call me Tessa. This is my best friend Chelsea," Tessa says, shaking her hand.

"I was just telling your mother how amazing your little community looks. I mean, with such limited resources, you've done quite well for yourselves."

"Yes, well, we've had some excellent leaders," Tessa says proudly. *And our resources aren't that limited.*

"Indeed, you have," Rene says dryly. "I'm sure you'll be next in line right? Is that how you pick your leaders here, through bloodline only?"

"It takes a little more than that," Tessa says defensively. "We choose who we think will be the best fit."

"How coincidental the best fit always has the same last name," Rene quips sarcastically. "I can't wait to learn more about your little village."

Say little one more time.

"How are your leaders chosen in Parish Two?" Chelsea asks, picking up the tension between them.

"Much like the mainland," Rene says with a smirk. "Through money and power."

"I see," Chelsea says, not sure what to ask next.

"I have to be going, but let's talk more during Vilë, I want to know everything there is to know about you and your family—neighbor," she smiles at them and walks away.

"And then there's her," Chelsea says, as soon as Rene is out of earshot. "I don't trust her."

"You and me both."

⇔⇔⇔⇔⇔⇔⇔⇔

Edmond gets back on the stage with a champagne glass. He taps it with a small fork a few times to quiet the hall and get everyone's attention. "Everyone, before we disperse, I wanted to do a little something for my darling daughter."

Here we go. Edmond gestures for Tessa to walk over to the mic. "Some of you may not know this, but today is her 16th birthday. So, ah, one and a two and one, two, three, four!"

The entire hall breaks out into a rendition of the birthday song, accompanied by the traditional drums. Tessa smiles awkwardly, trying not to show her embarrassment. Her mother rolls in a small dessert trolley with the cake she made.

"I made this cake for her," Joanna says proudly. "Everyone, come get a small slice!"

The cake is passed around among the dozens of remaining guests. Everyone gets a piece except for Tessa. *Typical.*

"Here, I saved you some of mine," Chelsea says. They walk over to a corner of the hall so she can eat it.

"Feeling any tingly sensations yet?" Chelsea asks. "Isn't it almost time?"

"I think it's just acid reflux."

Chelsea laughs loudly, causing some of the guests to turn their heads toward them. Joanna walks over to their corner in a hurry.

"Fun's over now," Chelsea whispers.

"Tessa! I told you before, you can't just sit in the corner with Chelsea all night. Come say hello to some of our guests, don't be rude," Joanna scolds.

"Hello to you too, Aunty Joanna," Chelsea says dryly.

"Chelsea, you know what I mean. You two have been joined at the hip since you were little. You can go a few minutes without each other."

Joanna pulls Tessa back toward the crowd.

"Text me later," Chelsea hisses to her.

Tessa nods. "I'll tell you everything."

JOANNA

He didn't even consider telling me. The thought never crossed his mind. Joanna shuffles her weight from one leg to the next, feigning interest in the mundane conversation between her women's empowerment group board members. They're all gathered in a circle, eating cake off small silver plates. "Was that buttercream you used for the frosting?" one of the women comments. "You must tell me the recipe."

Joanna smiles politely. "It *was* buttercream, something I whipped up from Edmond's grandmother's pages. I'll share it with the women's group later this week."

The other women nod in agreement. *And with no information, what am I to say when it comes up?*

"I can't believe little Tessa is already 16. She's grown up so fast," another board member comments. "You guys must be so proud."

"We are, she's an exceptional young woman."

Everyone nods in agreement again. *It's only a matter of time now.*

"So, when did you meet with Rene and Parish Two?" A woman from the back of the group asks casually. Everyone looks up from their plates to listen to Joanna's answer.

He didn't leave me a breadcrumb to work with.

"You know, we weren't sure how everyone would take it," Joanna says, not missing a beat. "So, we decided it's time for a joint effort, something that will leave a lasting legacy for the island."

"How do you plan to bring down the barrier?" asks the same woman in the back. "How would you even do that, through this supposed tunnel?"

Everyone turns to look at Joanna again.

"The entire plan will be laid out at the next Parish meeting," she lies. "Some things are still being worked out, but I promise everything will be discussed." She looks over at the grandfather clock in the front of the banquet hall. "I think it's time to wrap everything up, so I'll see everyone then. Thank you so much for coming!" Joanna moves around the circle, giving everyone a hug before she walks away. She spots Edmond from across the room talking to Brooks and strides over to him gracefully.

How could you embarrass me like this?

"Brooks, so lovely to see you," Joanna says smoothly. She pivots to Edmond. "Can we talk outside, please?"

"Let me say goodbye to everyone first. I'll meet you in the car," Edmond says matter-of-factly.

Joanna walks away, going through a side door of the banquet hall, eventually making it down the long stone steps of The Colosseum. The family town car is waiting at the bottom of the steps

"How was your evening, Joanna?" Taino asks.

"Tiring. Play some music for me, Taino."

Taino turns on the radio. A full hour goes by before Edmond gets in the car, Tessa is right behind him.

"What the hell is going on?"

EDMOND

"The council set up the first meeting," Edmond says convincingly. "These were dad's dying wishes like I said at the table. They just told me about it last minute."

Joanna doesn't respond, her eyes are fixed outside the window, watching the buildings flash by as they make their way home. Tessa shifts uncomfortably in her seat in front of him, trying hard not to make eye contact.

"Why would grandpa want something like this?" Tessa asks, her voice barely above a murmur. "Seems strange."

"Fantastic point, Tessa," Joanna says, still not taking her eyes from the window. "Sounds like a half-truth at best."

Edmond breathes deeply, ignoring Tessa's question. *You're mad because I didn't include you, you forget I don't need your approval, Jojo.* He runs his hands over her arms, switching tactics. "Are you going to stay mad all night?" Edmond asks, caressing her arm softly. Her skin reacts with tiny goosebumps, but Joanna does not respond to him. He scoots in a little closer to her.

"Just remember, I'm still in the car," Tessa says, watching her father's movements closely.

"How are you feeling, Tessa?" Joanna asks suddenly. "Is there any kind of ripping or burning feeling in your stomach?"

"No, should there be?"

"Everyone feels differently, but you should be feeling something," Edmond says. "Not even a prickle?"

Tessa furrows her brow. "Does this mean I'm not turning?"

Don't sound so excited about it.

"Not necessarily." Edmond checks his watch. "It's only 11:30pm, still lots of time for something to happen."

The trio say nothing else for the rest of the car ride. Joanna remains unresponsive to all of Edmond's advances. *A lie is better than the truth.* Edmond repeats to himself. *We're running out of money; we need their help. We need that weapon.*

The driver pulls into their horseshoe driveway. Tessa gets out of the car first. "I'm going to call Chelsea while I'm still normal," she declares.

"Don't say that," Edmond says sharply. "It's a great honor to have this gift, call your Uncle Seven. He should be here for this as well."

Tessa nods and walks up the driveway, leaving Edmond and Joanna alone in the car.

"Taino, can you excuse us for a moment?" Joanna asks.

"Of course, Joanna." Taino gets out of the car and walks toward the house.

"You made me look like an absolute idiot," Joanna seethes. "How could you not tell me any of this? When did you meet with her?"

"I'm just executing the plan that was set in place by the council, it's what my dad wanted apparently."

Joanna turns to look at him for the first time since they got in the car. "Liar."

Edmond doesn't respond.

"Isaiah would have never planned this, he *hated* them. You had her at our altar, he will never forgive you for this."

I don't need his forgiveness.

"I think this change will be healthy for everyone, there's no reason for Parish Two to be our enemy."

Joanna narrows her eyes at him. "Why didn't you tell me this before then?"

"It all happened very quickly. I wasn't even sure if they would agree. It all got finalized yesterday," Edmond says smoothly.

"Where did you meet?" Joanna demands.

Edmond rubs the back of his neck and shoulders, feeling the full weight of the day on his back. "This is the first time we met. I communicated through the boy pigeon."

"How many people knew about this besides the carrier pigeon?" she stares into his face, hungry to catch him in a lie.

"Just Brooks, that's it."

"I thought you just said the council set up the meeting?" Joanna says.

"Yes, but I followed through on everything, they know very little." Edmond tries to make his face blank but he can tell from Joanna's body language she doesn't believe him.

She exhales slowly, opening the car door. "This conversation isn't over. I can't believe you didn't consider telling me anything about this. There's a tunnel in the barrier and we're making nice with our sworn enemies, for what?" She shakes her head and chuckles. "You really think you can trust her? Don't you remember what Nanzi said?"

"I made a decision for the betterment of my people. Jojo, this is something *we need*. You don't understand." Edmond pleads with her.

Joanna shrugs away his hand. "No, Edmond, this is something *you wanted*. I hope you are prepared for the consequences."

She gets out of the car and walks up the driveway, Edmond follows after her.

I'm prepared for anything. This victory will be my legacy.

CONTESSA

Tap, tap, tap. Tap, tap, tap. Tessa checks the window again, to detect where the sound is coming from. When she draws back her curtains she doesn't see anything. She strains her eyes, trying to penetrate the darkness. Nothing.

"Doesn't anyone else hear that?" she asks the adults in her room. "Something keeps tapping at the window."

"Probably just lose debris flying around or something," Joanna says from the corner of the room. She props the book she has on her lap open. "You need to focus, it will be any minute now."

Edmond groans a little, rolling over onto the other side of the bed. "Did I miss anything?"

Tessa shakes her head. "Nothing yet," she keeps her curtains open, moving away from the window. Seven walks into the room a few moments later carrying a tray full of teacups.

"I made lemongrass tea for everyone," Seven says proudly. "Should help us stay up for the long night ahead."

"How long is this going to take?" Tessa asks nervously.

Edmond checks his watch, "It's almost 1:30 in the morning, happened for me around 3:00 am but I was showing signs early, the transition just took a while."

"I remember that morning, you wouldn't stop crying about the pain," Seven says, blowing on his tea.

Edmond smirks, taking one of the teacups from the tray. "That was one of the most intense bouts of pain I've ever experienced, I don't think there's anything like it."

"Try childbirth," Joanna quips, she also takes a teacup from the tray. "My transition wasn't that painful, it happened so fast I barely remember it."

"What should I expect?" Tessa asks, her nerves getting more frayed by the moment. "Will it hurt a lot?"

"Hard to say really, you're a lot older than anyone else who has turned in the family," Joanna says matter-of-factly.

Tap, tap, tap, tap.

Tessa turns her head towards the window. "You all hear that, right?"

She takes a few steps, squinting her eyes tightly. "What is that?" Suddenly, a hot burning sensation fills Tessa's body, rushing through her blood and through her bones. "AHHH!" she screams in pain and drops to her knees. She looks at her hands, watching in disbelief as her flesh pulls itself wider, she can hear her bones cracking, changing shape under her skin. "It's too much, it hurts too much!" she yells out.

Tap, tap, tap, tap.

The sound at the window is still incessant, filling in the silence between Tessa's painful cries.

"It's okay, Tess, it's okay." Her mother bends down next to her, rubbing her back. "It will be over soon, accept the pain. You have to."

Edmond stoops down on her other side. "Embrace it," he instructs carefully. "You can't be scared."

"SOMETHING IS TEARING ME APART," she screams at the top of her lungs. The feeling of five thousand tons of pressure hits Tessa on the back, her heart feels like it's about to tear itself out of her chest. *I can't do this! It's too much! It hurts so badly.* "Something's wrong," she says, panicking. "I can't handle it, I can't-"

"Bear through it," Seven says, kneeling down in front of her. "I know it hurts but it won't last forever." He takes a mint balm out of his pocket and rubs it under her nose. "Take a deep inhale of this and keep pushing."

Tessa grits her teeth, and getting a few sniffs of the balm calms her down for a moment. Her back makes one last cracking sound and her hands start to grow fur.

Tap, tap, tap, tap, *ping!*

Tessa's window fractures in the middle, something outside is refusing to be ignored.

"Something isn't right," Tessa says, feeling the panic rise in her chest again. "What is that outside, what does it want?"

She moves a few inches closer to the window, her parents hold their hands out as a safety net around her.

"Don't worry about that," Seven says, moving out of her way. "Focus on the change happening within you, see it through to the end."

Ping, ping, ping.

Dark brown fur creeps over Tessa's body, she catches a reflection of herself in the mirror and pauses. *It's really happening.* Blood starts dripping out of her mouth onto her carpet, as sharp fangs violently rip out of her gums. Tessa growls again, feeling another wave of pain sear through her body. She spits out some of the blood. The taste of her dinner mixed with metal, and the mint balm, churn in her stomach. "I can't breathe. I need air." She takes the final few steps towards the window, the second she releases the latch the window assailant is revealed. A strange bird, the size of an eagle leaps through the window, clawing and scratching at Tessa.

"Get it off of her!" Joanna screams, turning into her wolf form instantly. She waves her paws towards the bird, clawing at its feathers. The bird screeches in protest but remains focused on Tessa, digging its talons deep into her flesh until it draws blood.

Edmond and Seven transition into wolf form and strategically move on either side of the bird. Edmond nods his head three times and Seven hooks his claws under the belly of the bird while Edmond simultaneously grabs it by the neck. They both press down on the animal. Edmond motions his head toward the open window, ignoring the bird's loud squawking protests. They shuffle over and throw the dying animal below.

Tessa groans in pain on the floor nursing her wound, feeling the pain of the transformation subside. She feels the fur all over her face and arms, knowing instinctively something is off.

"It cut you deep," Joanna says looking at her arm, "are you okay?"

She tries to respond but no words come out.

Joanna, Seven and Edmond revert back to their human forms. "You can't speak while you're in animal form," Edmond says smiling. "It takes some time getting used to but you learn to communicate with body language and hand signals."

Tessa nods her head, showing she understands, a tingly surge comes through her chest. *Something is wrong.* She whimpers at her parents, scratching at her back.

"You have to change back," Joanna repeats to her. "We can't understand you."

Tessa makes a yapping sound at them, still trying to communicate her distress.

"We don't know what you're trying to say," Seven says gently. "You have to-" he snaps his mouth shut suddenly, noticing something growing behind her. "Wait, what is that?"

Tessa keeps scratching at her back, feeling two sharp prongs growing out of her fur.

Joanna, Seven and Edmond watch in horror as two large black and gray wings fully form on her back.

Tessa turns towards her mirror and screams in horror and disbelief.

Born in London and raised in Antigua and Barbuda, Amina Lovell's debut trilogy *Opal Island* is based on her Caribbean upbringing and West African folklore. Before she started writing young adult fiction, she was a television news producer for three and a half years after attending The School of Journalism at Columbia University. In the spring of 2018, she decided to quit her production job and pursue writing full-time. Amina is a lover of adult animation, tattoos, and long hikes. She currently lives in Los Angeles, California.

You can visit her online at aminalovell.com

ABOUT THE EDITOR

Angela Benson is the Co-founder of Bee Infinite Publishing. She was born and raised in the Los Angeles area and is a graduate of UCLA. Angela has been an educator, school administrator, and an educational consultant in the public and private sector for over 25 years. She has experience in the publishing industry with such companies as McGraw-Hill. She is the author of the forthcoming children's book, *Princess Nile & The Lotus Fairy*, an intergenerational journey of self-discovery, joy, and adventure. She spearheads the editing, proofreading, and creative development of Bee Infinite projects. Angela is an art collector and a lover of first-edition books. She resides with her family in her historic Craftsman home based in Los Angeles, California.

ABOUT THE ILLUSTRATOR

Kai Adia is the Co-founder of Bee Infinite Publishing, spearheading the editing and creative design of innovative book projects that amplify BIPOC voices. She is a writer of prose poetry and short stories, focusing on the genres of science fiction and fantasy. In 2020, she published, designed, and illustrated her debut poetry collection, *The Depths of Anima* (Bee Infinite Publishing). In 2018, she graduated from Pitzer College with a Bachelor of Arts degree in Environmental Analysis and English & World Literature. In 2017, she was awarded the Bea Matas Hollfelder '87 Award by the English Department at Pitzer College for exceptional creative writing and literature. She has shared her work in various journals and anthologies, including *The New Brownies' Book: A Love Letter to Black Families* (Chronicle Books) and *Future Splendor: Celebrating a New Renaissance* (Bee Infinite Publishing). Kai is also an experienced copywriter and editor, working with organizations like Habitat for Humanity of Greater Los Angeles, the Pan African Film Festival, Stocker Street Creative, American Wheelman, Formula 1 Racing X Smartsheet, and The Hidden Genius Project. When Kai isn't writing, she drinks jasmine green tea and watches too many Kdramas.

BEE INFINITE PUBLISHING

As a Black women-owned and operated space, we hold an Afrofuturist perspective at the core of our business. We're committed to amplifying the voices and stories of people of color, especially Black and Indigenous voices. Our books honor the infinite artistry of our collective community through the creative lens of compelling storytelling.

Our mission is to be an equitable, conscious publishing house. We want to put creative ownership back into the hands of those who dream of fantastical new worlds, who think in verse, and who draw when holding a pen.

Learn more about our books, projects, and products at www.beeinfinite.org.

Let's Connect!
Instagram: @beeinfinite_publishing
Twitter: @beeinfinite_

CPSIA information can be obtained
at www.ICGtesting.com
Printed in the USA
JSHW021915230223
38153JS00001B/4